Sky Lanterns

EGMONT

We bring stories to life

First published in Great Britain in 2013
by Egmont UK Limited, The Yellow Building,
1 Nicholas Road, London W11 4AN

ISBN 978 1 4052 6985 8
56317/2

It was Chinese New Year and the children were very excited. They were making Chinese sky lanterns to fly over Pontpandy!

"I want to launch mine **NOW,**" cried Norman Price.

His teacher Mrs Chen sighed. "You need to decorate it first," she said.

At the Railway Station, Elvis was testing Bessie's new hose. The hose squirted out foam to stop fires from spreading.

"This is more difficult than I expected," said Elvis, fiddling with the equipment. **WHOOSH!** Sticky foam squirted out of the hose, covering him from head to toe!

Meanwhile, Mrs Chen and the children had arrived at the Railway Station with their decorated lanterns. Fireman Sam was waiting for them.

"When can we fly our lanterns?" asked Norman.

"Soon, but we need to take them to the right place …" said Mrs Chen.

"Yes, they have to be launched somewhere safe!" Sam reminded them.

Just then, Gareth tooted the whistle of the train.

"**All aboard!**" he called.

Mrs Chen smiled. "We're going to release the lanterns ... in the mountains," she revealed.

Everyone cheered! It was the perfect place for the launch.

It was a long trip up the mountain, and the children were very excited when they arrived.

"**At last!**" cried Norman, leaping off the train.

But just as Gareth lit their lanterns, Moose from the Mountain Activity Centre arrived.

"Fireman Sam called me," Moose said. "The wind has changed direction. It isn't safe to fly your lanterns here anymore."

"But they're all ready to go ..." moaned Norman. And before anyone could stop him, he let his lantern go!

"**Oooh!**" cooed Norman, staring up at the drifting light. "Isn't it beautiful?"

"It's not beautiful!" said Moose crossly. "**It's dangerous!**"

The wind had blown the lantern into the forest. Tree branches began to catch fire.

"I'd better call Fireman Sam," cried Moose in alarm.

Moments later, Moose's call came through at the Fire Station.

"There's a forest fire up in the mountains!" called out Officer Steele. "I think we need Tom Thomas' helicopter and Bessie for this one!"

Tom Thomas arrived at the scene first.

SWOOSH! He released the water over the flames – but the fire still kept on spreading.

"It's moving too quickly!" he warned Sam over the radio. **"It's heading straight for the kids!"**

At that moment, Bessie reached the mountaintop.

"Time to try out our new sticky foam!" ordered Sam.

"Right you are," said Elvis.

He took careful aim with the hose, and Penny flicked the switch. **WHOOOOOOSH!**

A jet of foam shot out, stopping the fire in its tracks!

Later, back at the Railway Station, Fireman
Sam invited everyone to come and launch their
lanterns safely.

"Nothing dangerous nearby, wind blowing gently
and in the right direction," said Fireman Sam.
"You're clear to go!"

One by one, the children finally released their
lanterns into the sky ... It was magical!

 The End